The Sleepover Club

Have you been invited to all these sleepovers?

Vive le Sleepover Club!

by Narinder Dhami

(((Collins

📖 *An imprint of HarperCollinsPublishers*

The Sleepover Club ® is a
registered trademark of HarperCollins*Publishers* Ltd

First published in Great Britain by Collins in 2000
Collins is an imprint of HarperCollins*Publishers* Ltd
77-85 Fulham Palace Road, Hammersmith,
London, W6 8JB

The HarperCollins website address is
www.**fire**and**water**.com

3 5 7 9 8 6 4 2

Text copyright © Narinder Dhami 2000

Original series characters, plotlines
and settings © Rose Impey 1997

ISBN 0 00 675501-1

The author asserts the moral right to
be identified as the author of the work.

Printed and bound in Great Britain by
Omnia Books Limited,
Glasgow

Sleepover Kit List

1. Sleeping bag
2. Pillow
3. Pyjamas or a nightdress
4. Slippers
5. Toothbrush, toothpaste, soap etc
6. Towel
7. Teddy
8. A creepy story
9. Food for a midnight feast:
   chocolate, crisps, sweets, biscuits.
   In fact anything you like to eat.
10. Torch
11. Hairbrush
12. Hair things like a bobble or hairband,
    if you need them
13. Clean knickers and socks
14. Change of clothes for the next day
15. Sleepover diary and membership card

CHAPTER ONE

Salut tout le monde! Je m'appelle Rosie, et j'ai une super histoire à vous raconter sur les vacances du Sleepover Club à Paris!

No, don't get your knickers in a twist – you haven't picked up the wrong book! The Sleepover Club have kind of gone all French, because last half-term we went on a school trip to Paris. We had a really cool time, but as you can probably guess by now, things didn't go all that smoothly. In fact, just about everything that could go wrong did! But I'd better start right at the beginning…

The beginning was at school a few months ago in Cuddington, the village where we all live. The bell had just rung for hometime, and the Sleepover Club were all desperate to get out of school as fast as we could, as usual. You remember the Sleepover Club, don't you? There's Frankie, Kenny, Fliss, Lyndz and me (Rosie), and we sleep over at each other's houses at the weekends.

"What's up with Weaver?" Kenny said crossly as Mrs Weaver started rooting around in her desk instead of letting us go. "I want to go home!"

Everyone in the class started muttering and moaning, until Mrs Weaver glanced up and fixed everyone with a beady glare. Then we all shut up.

"Sorry to keep you waiting," she said, picking up a pile of papers. "But I have some letters for your parents here."

"Boring!" Frankie whispered with a huge yawn.

"The school is organising a trip to Paris next half-term for this year group," Mrs

Weaver went on. "And we need to know how many of you would be interested in going."

Well, *that* wasn't boring! We all looked at each other in delight. Our last school trip abroad, to Spain, had been cool – and we were all up for some more!

"Excellent!" Kenny said. "I'm definitely going!"

"Me too!" I put in.

"I'm going to ask my mum and dad if I can go," Lyndz added.

"I wonder if we get to go to Disneyland Paris?" Frankie asked, looking excited.

"Oh, I've been there," said Fliss. "It's fab!"

As you can probably guess by now, we were all determined to go! And there was one other special reason why we were looking forward to it. We've kind of started having sleepovers in different places whenever we can. We've had one in a museum, one when we were camping and one when we went on the last school trip to Spain. Now we had the chance to have a sleepover in France – and none of us was going to miss *that*!

*   *   *

"When are we going to have our French sleepover then?"

Kenny said that in a really loud voice while we were waiting in the school minibus to go through the Channel Tunnel to Paris. Immediately we all started shushing her, and looking round to check where Mrs Weaver was.

"Shut up, Kenny!" hissed Frankie.

"Yeah, shut up, Bigmouth!" Lyndz added.

"If Mrs Weaver hears that, she'll go ballistic," Fliss said nervously. "After the school trip to Spain, I bet she watches us all the time."

"Do you remember when Mrs Weaver caught us right in the middle of the Spanish sleepover?" Kenny grinned. "She looked pretty spooky in her nightie!"

"Ssh!" said Fliss, even though she was giggling as hard as the rest of us. Luckily Mrs Weaver was down at the front of the minibus with Mrs Jackson and Mr Tate, who were the other teachers coming with us. We were near the back of the minibus, although we hadn't managed to bag the back seat. Kenny was sitting next to Frankie, Fliss and Lyndz were sitting behind them, and I was behind Fliss and Lyndz.

"We won't get caught this time," Frankie said confidently.

"Maybe we'll all be in the same room," Lyndz said hopefully. "That'd make it easier."

"What are we going to do at a French sleepover anyway?" I asked.

"Eat snails!" Kenny suggested with an evil gleam in her eye.

"Urgh! No way!" Fliss turned pale.

"Do you know what 'snail' is in French?" Frankie asked, pulling a French phrasebook out of her bag. We all groaned loudly.

"Oh, you're not going to bore us to death again, are you!" Kenny moaned. When we went to Spain, Frankie took a Spanish dictionary and kept on telling us loads of stupid words.

Frankie flipped through the book, ignoring the lot of us. "*Escargot*," she said, "That's French for snail."

"Well, I'm not eating any *escargots* at our sleepover," Fliss said firmly.

"We could have French bread and cheese," Lyndz suggested.

"And onions," I added.

"Hey, I've got a great idea!" Kenny announced. "We can dance the Can-Can!"

"Don't you have to show your knickers when you do the Can-Can?" Fliss giggled.

"That depends on how high you can kick!" Kenny started humming the Can-Can tune, and kicking up her legs against the seat in front of her. "Da, da, de-de-de-de da, da!"

"Do you mind, Laura McKenzie!" Emma Hughes bounced up out of the seat in front of Kenny, and glared at her. "You're kicking me!"

"Well, I don't have a problem with that!" Kenny retorted coolly, and the rest of us fell about.

"Stop it, or we'll tell Mrs Weaver!" Emily Berryman's head appeared over the top of the seats too. Yup, the M&Ms were out in force. You've got to remember the M&Ms. They're our biggest enemies in the whole world! We call them the Queen and the Goblin because Emma's so snooty, and Emily's small and weedy with a deep voice. They are both major pains.

Kenny pulled one of her most gruesome faces at the M&Ms, and they both sniffed and turned their backs on us. Then the Queen bent down and pulled her bag from under her seat. Emma had brought about four pieces of luggage with her – and they all matched. Talk about posh!

"Do you want a Twix, Emily?" she asked.

"Pity they had to come with us," Frankie muttered as Emma opened her bag. "We had a great time in Spain without them!"

"Yeah, it was cool!" I agreed. "What's French for 'The M&Ms are a complete pain in the behind', Frankie?"

Frankie grinned. "I don't think that'll be in my phrasebook!"

"I hope we don't have to go to loads and loads of boring museums in Paris!" Fliss moaned, passing round a bag of fun-size Wispa bars. "You know what teachers are like!"

"I bet there's lots of interesting things to see, though," Lyndz said.

"Oh, rats to boring museums!" Kenny bounced up and down in her seat. "I can't wait to go to Disneyland Paris!"

We all started talking at once then. We were going to be in Paris for four days, and we were spending the very last day at Disneyland. We were all dying to see it, and go on all the best rides.

"Space Mountain is awesome." Fliss looked a bit superior. She's been to Disneyland Paris *and* Disneyworld in Florida. She goes on loads of holidays with her mum, her brother Callum and her mum's boyfriend Andy. "And the parade of Disney characters is really cool too."

"I want to see Honey, I Shrunk The Audience!" Frankie said. "That's new, isn't it?"

Fliss nodded. "That wasn't there when I went."

"Can I have a bit of quiet, please?" called Mrs Weaver, who was standing at the front of the minibus and waving her clipboard. We all shut up reluctantly to listen. We didn't want to get on the wrong side of Mrs Weaver right from the start!

"Now, we'll be boarding the train which will take us through the Channel Tunnel in about ten minutes," Mrs Weaver went on. "Before we do, I've got something very important to say to you all."

"Oh, here it comes!" Kenny groaned, "The Big Lecture!"

"Did you want to say something, Laura?" Mrs Weaver glared down the minibus in our direction.

"No, Miss," Kenny muttered, and the M&Ms sniggered.

"Right, it goes without saying that I expect all of you to be on your very best behaviour." Mrs Weaver glanced in our direction again. I don't know why. "When you're abroad, you are representing your country as well as your school, and we want to make a good impression, so..."

Kenny wasn't listening. Suddenly she bent down in her seat, so that me, Fliss and

Lyndz, who were behind her, couldn't see what she was doing.

"What's up with Kenny?" Lyndz hissed.

"Maybe she's fainted!" Fliss giggled.

"Ssh!" Frankie turned round and winked at us. "Pass it on!"

We didn't have a clue what was going on – until suddenly one of Emma's posh leather bags appeared from under Kenny's seat! Emma had been showing off about her matching luggage, and she'd put the smallest bag under her seat. Now Lyndz, who was sitting behind Kenny, bent down and pushed the bag backwards to me.

"Pass it on, Rosie!" she whispered.

I grabbed the bag and shoved it under my seat. Meanwhile, we all sat there listening to Mrs Weaver, and trying not to laugh.

"And although we want you to have a good time, there are a few important rules you all have to remember," Mrs Weaver was saying sternly.

"My bag!" Emma Hughes jumped up from her seat. "Mrs Weaver, my bag's gone!"

Kenny turned round and nodded to me, so I immediately pushed the bag back under the seat to Lyndz, who quickly pushed it back to Kenny. By the time Mrs Weaver made it to the back of the minibus, we were all sitting there, looking as if butter wouldn't melt in our mouths.

"Where did you put your bag, Emma?" Mrs Weaver raised her eyebrows.

"Under my seat, Miss!" Emma said furiously, "And I bet I know who's taken it too!" She turned round and glared at Kenny.

"Well, thanks very much!" Kenny said indignantly, and we all nearly bust a gut trying not to laugh.

Mrs Weaver bent down and looked under the Queen's seat. "Is that the bag you're looking for?" she asked in a frosty voice.

Emma bent over and took a look. "Er… yes!" she stammered. "But it wasn't there before!" She jumped up from her seat, eyes narrowed, and shot Kenny an evil stare. "You took it!"

"No way!" Kenny retorted airily.

"Hm, well, no harm done as you've got the bag back safely, Emma." But Mrs Weaver fixed us with a beady-eyed glare. "I hope you girls have been listening to what I've been saying? I want you all on your best behaviour and doing what you're told *without any exceptions*. Do I make myself clear?"

"Yes, Mrs Weaver," we all chorused.

Mrs Weaver turned round and went back to the front of the bus.

Straightaway Kenny turned round and winked at the rest of us. "But that won't stop us having the biggest sleepover of all time, will it!"

CHAPTER TWO

"We're in!" Kenny yelled, grabbing the last Wispa bar from under Fliss's nose. "Just think, there's thousands and thousands of tons of water over our heads right at this very moment!"

"Oh, shut up, Kenny!" said Fliss. The train had just entered the Channel Tunnel, and everyone on the minibus had started whooping and cheering.

"You look a bit green, Fliss," I said sympathetically.

"She'd look a lot greener if we were on top

of the water instead of underneath it!" Kenny remarked, screwing up her chocolate wrapper. She leaned over the seat and dropped it gently on top of Emma's head. Emma was talking to Emily and didn't notice. "I wonder what would happen if the tunnel collapsed, and all the water came pouring in?"

"The French word for water is *eau*," said Frankie, who had her nose in her phrasebook again. "Pronounced 'oh'."

Kenny clasped her hands and pretended to look scared. "*Eau* no! I'm up to my eyeballs in *eau*!"

"Oh, shut up, Kenny!" Fliss wailed, looking even greener, although she was giggling too. "The tunnel isn't going to collapse on us!"

"It'd be just like *Titanic*, only worse!" Frankie said with a grin.

"Fliss wouldn't mind if Leonardo DiCaprio came to save her!" Lyndz remarked, and we all fell about, even Fliss.

"Eek!" Emma Hughes had just realised that there was something on top of her hair, and she was shaking her head around like crazy. "Emily, is that a spider in my hair?"

"Keep still," Emily instructed her, while the Sleepover Club chortled behind their seats. "No, it's a Wispa wrapper!"

"What?" Emma shot to her feet, her face bright pink, and threw the wrapper back over the seats at Kenny. "You're so childish, Laura McKenzie!"

"Me!" Kenny exclaimed. "How do you know it was *me*?"

Emma gave her a haughty stare, and then leaned across the aisle. Alana Banana Palmer was sitting in the seat opposite. She's kind of a mate of the M&Ms, so that makes her kind of our enemy too. But we don't exactly worry about her too much. Alana Banana's too dozy to scare anyone!

"Alana, change seats with me and Emily," Emma ordered.

"OK." Alana Banana didn't even bother arguing with Emma. She picked her bag up off the seat next to her, got up and moved across the aisle. Meanwhile, Emily and

Emma picked up their bags too, and, giving us a smug look, switched seats.

"I could put a thousand Wispa wrappers on Alana's head, and she's so snoozy she wouldn't notice!" Kenny whispered as Alana settled herself into the seat in front of her.

We all started laughing. Then Emma suddenly jumped to her feet again.

"Urggh! There's chewing gum stuck on this seat!" she squealed, trying to look over her shoulder at her backside.

We all bounced up to have a look – and sure enough, there was a large wodge of pink chewing gum stuck to the back of Emma's pedal-pushers. It looked like it had been well chewed too! We all roared.

"Alana, it must have been stuck to the bottom of your bag!" Emma snapped, her face as pink as the chewing gum.

"Oh, was it?" Alana said dozily.

"Nice one, Alana!" Kenny called, giving her a thumbs-up, and the Queen looked fit to bust.

The rest of the tunnel journey was pretty

boring, because the teachers wouldn't let us get off the minibus and explore, but at least it was only thirty-five minutes. Soon we were out of the tunnel and into the sunshine again, racing through the French countryside along the motorway.

"We're in France!" Frankie announced. But although the countryside was quite pretty, it didn't look that different from England. Anyway, motorways are the same boring concrete things wherever you go, aren't they?

We were all getting a bit restless when suddenly Lyndz had a brill idea.

"The first person to spot the Eiffel Tower gets fifty pee – I mean fifty francs – from the rest of us!" she said.

"Fifty francs! Wow!" Frankie's eyes lit up.

Lyndz looked a bit worried. "Why? How much is that?"

"About five pounds!" Frankie said with a grin.

"OK, ten francs then!" Lyndz said firmly.

Well, that made it a bit more interesting!

We all started looking at the roadsigns then, checking how many more kilometres it was to Paris. As we got closer and closer, we were all straining our eyes to get that first important look at the Eiffel Tower.

"There it is!" shouted Fliss, Lyndz and Kenny together as suddenly the Tower appeared in the distance!

Paris looked amazing. We couldn't stop yelling and pointing out things to each other.

"Look!" Fliss squealed. "Look at all the shops! Look at all the designer labels!"

"There's the Eiffel Tower again!" Kenny yelled, bouncing up and down in a frenzy.

"Where?" we all yelled back.

"There's the River What-do-you-call-it!" I pointed out.

"The River Seine, actually!" Emma put in snootily, but we ignored her.

By the time we got to the hotel where we were staying, we were all well excited. Mrs Weaver was shooting everyone some pretty fierce glares as we drew up outside the hotel, and Mr Tate, who was driving the minibus, looked a bit of a nervous wreck. The traffic in Paris was pretty awesome!

"Right, our hotel should be just down here," Mrs Weaver said.

We peered down the narrow side-street – and then we all did a double-take, including the teachers. The hotel was a tall, scary-looking old house with big high windows, and a massive wooden door. It looked like something out of *The Addams Family*.

"Is that it?" Fliss gasped. "It looks horrible!"

"Maybe it's ha-au-au-au-aunted!" Kenny grinned and winked at the rest of us.

"I'm sure it's very nice," said Mrs Weaver firmly as the minibus drew to a halt. "No, stay where you are, please! I'm going to tell the owner, Madame Dupont, that we have arrived."

"I wish we were staying somewhere else," Fliss shivered as Mrs Weaver climbed off the coach. You know what Fliss is like about scary, spooky places and stuff!

"Nah, it'll be good!" Kenny assured her.

"I bet there's some old attics right at the top of the house – we might find a brilliant place to have a big sleepover party!"

Fliss groaned, and Lyndz wasn't looking too thrilled either. Neither was I, actually. The house really did look spooky.

Just then, a woman in a maid's uniform came outside to put a bag of rubbish in the bin. Frankie giggled.

"Check her out!"

The maid *looked* like one of the Addams Family! She was tall and bony, with a grim face and bushy black eyebrows. She saw us all sitting on the minibus, but she didn't smile. She just dropped the rubbish in the bin, and stomped back inside.

"I don't like it here!" Fliss whispered, looking even more panicked. Right at that moment, though, Mrs Weaver came out again.

"Stay where you are until I call your names, please." She consulted her clipboard. "Laura, Frankie, Felicity, Lyndsey and Rosie, you get off first, please." Grinning smugly at the M&Ms, we picked up our bags and rushed off the minibus.

"You're in a room together on the top floor," Mrs Weaver went on, and we all glanced at each other in delight. Being in a room together would make it really easy to have a brilliant sleepover! Only Fliss didn't look too thrilled.

"The top floor?" she said in a wobbly voice. "We're not in an old and dusty attic, are we?"

Mrs Weaver frowned. "Of course not, Felicity! Now here's Pascal, who's the son of the owner…"

A boy with dark hair came out of the hotel entrance. He was about a year or so older than us, and quite good-looking, I suppose – if you like boys!

"He's going to show you the way to your room."

"Oh, right!" said Fliss, brightening up a bit. She pretends she doesn't like boys that much, but she's not a very good fibber!

"*Bonjour*," said Pascal.

"*Bonjour*," we all chorused. That was about all the French we knew!

27

"At least he looks normal!" Kenny remarked as we followed him into the big hotel lobby. "Not like that scary maid with the caterpillar eyebrows!"

"Ssh!" Lyndz nudged her. "He might understand what you're saying!"

"Oh, I bet he doesn't speak English." Kenny winked at us, then turned to Pascal. "Do you speak English?"

Pascal shrugged. "*Je ne comprends pas.*"

"What does that mean?" I asked.

"You know English?" Kenny repeated, waving her hands around.

Pascal shook his head.

"He doesn't!" Kenny said triumphantly. "Maybe we should teach him some. Hey, Pascal! Say 'Leicester City are the best football team in the whole world'!"

Pascal grinned. "Leicester Ceety..." he began, then he stopped and looked puzzled.

"That's too hard for him, Kenny!" Frankie said impatiently. "Hey, Pascal, say 'Emma Hughes stinks'!"

"Emma Yoos steenks," said Pascal

obediently, and we all roared with laughter.

The hotel was OK inside. At least it wasn't *too* much like a haunted house! All the furniture and the wallpaper was really old-fashioned, but it was very clean. Fliss cheered up a bit, but her face soon fell again as Pascal led us up three dark, gloomy flights of stairs to our bedroom.

The bedroom was quite nice. It had a double bed and three singles, all crammed in together. There were flowery quilts on the bed, and matching curtains at the window, which gave us a brilliant view over the rooftops of Paris. We could even see the Eiffel Tower in the distance.

"Who's sharing?" Kenny asked, bouncing up and down on the double bed.

"I'm not sleeping with Lyndz – she hiccups in the night!" said Fliss immediately.

"I'm not sleeping with Kenny – she's got freezing feet!" I put in.

"I'm not sleeping with Fliss – she snores!" Frankie said. "Sometimes," she added, as Fliss gave her a furious look.

"I'll share with Lyndz," Kenny suggested. "Then if she hiccups in the night, I can put my cold feet on her and give her a shock!"

We all agreed, so Frankie, Fliss and I bagged one each of the single beds.

"Hey, Pascal!" Frankie called. "Say this – 'I've got a big spot on my bottom'!"

"I've got a beeg spot on my bottom!" Pascal repeated, looking very pleased with himself. We all tried not to laugh too hard in case he caught on.

"'Bye!" Kenny called as he went out. "Be careful how you sit down!"

We all fell about when the door closed.

"I think we're going to have some fun with Pascal!" Frankie spluttered.

Just then the door opened again and we all sat up. The scary maid stomped in, carrying two of our suitcases as if they were as light as a feather. She looked sourly at us, dropped the cases on the floor and went out again.

"Well, she's a right laugh, isn't she!" said Lyndz.

"She's spooky!" Fliss said with a shiver.

"Yeah, maybe she's really a zombie!" Kenny suggested eagerly. "Maybe she'll creep into our room at night and—"

"Kenny!" Fliss wailed. "Is there a lock on the door?"

We all rushed over to have a look. But then we noticed something else. Just past our door, there was another long, dusty, winding staircase, which went up right over our heads and then wound out of sight.

"Wow!" Kenny breathed. "That must go right up to the attic. Let's go and take a look!"

Fliss didn't look too happy, and I wasn't that keen myself. Meanwhile Lyndz was looking at a sign on the wall.

"*Entrée interdite au public*," she read. "What does that mean?"

"Maybe it means – *this way to the haunted attic*!" Kenny suggested, with a wicked gleam in her eye.

"No, it doesn't." Frankie had gone back into the bedroom to get her phrasebook. "It means we can't go up there. It's private."

Fliss looked relieved.

"Oh, well…" Kenny grinned round at us. "We'll just have to wait until tomorrow night when we have our first sleepover, won't we? Then we'll be able to explore!"

CHAPTER THREE

"I'm sure I heard noises coming from that attic last night!"

Frankie sat up in bed, rubbing her eyes. It was morning, and the sunshine was streaming through the windows. We all sat up in our beds and stared at her.

"You're making it up!" Fliss said fearfully.

I hadn't heard anything at all. By the time we'd unpacked and then had something to eat, we were all pretty tired and I'd slept really soundly.

"No, I did!" Frankie insisted. "It was just

after we'd gone to bed, but all the rest of you were snoring your heads off!"

"I reckon you're having us on," Kenny said.

"No, I'm not!" Frankie insisted, but we all chucked our pillows in her direction and then jumped on her.

We were starving, so we dashed down to breakfast at eight o'clock sharp. The rest of the school party were just coming in too, along with the teachers, and there were a few other guests in the dining room, mostly Japanese and British tourists. We managed to bag a table on our own, well away from the M&Ms and the teachers.

"Hey, look!" said Kenny as the grim-faced maid, who was called Chantal, brought some plates over to our table. "Croissants! Brilliant!"

Chantal gave us a dirty look as we all dived on the plate of croissants.

"Mmm, this beats Coco-Pops and burnt toast any day!" Lyndz said through a mouthful of crumbs.

While we were eating, Pascal came in.

"Hi, Pascal! Over here!" Kenny waved at him, and he came over to our table. "How are you?"

Pascal nodded and smiled, obviously not understanding a word. "*Avez-vous bien dormi la nuit dernière?*"

We all looked blank.

"What's he saying?" Lyndz asked.

"Haven't a clue." I said.

Kenny tried again. "What – did – you – say – Pascal?" she said in a really slow voice, as if she was talking to a two-year-old.

"Oh, don't be daft, Kenny!" Frankie scoffed. "He's not going to understand, however slowly you speak!"

"Maybe we can ask Mrs Weaver," I suggested. "She speaks good French."

"Not a good idea, Rosie-Posie," said Kenny. "He might tell her some of the English we've been teaching him!"

We all giggled. Meanwhile, Pascal still looked a bit confused, although he was smiling.

"OK, Pascal, say this," Kenny told him gleefully. "'Mrs Weaver is a—'"

"Kenny!" we all hissed frantically. "She's coming over!"

"We're leaving at nine sharp for sightseeing, girls." Mrs Weaver stopped by our table as we stared innocently at her. "So make sure you're on the minibus by then."

"Yes, Mrs Weaver," we said together.

"That was close!" I breathed as the teacher went back to her table. "You'd better be careful what you teach Pascal, Kenny!"

"Hey, Pascal," Kenny said suddenly. "You know that staircase by our door – where does it go to?"

"*Comment?*" Pascal gave us a blank look.

"That staircase," Kenny began again, but Frankie nudged her.

"Give it up, Kenny!" she said. "He doesn't know what you're going on about!"

"Oh, well, we can find out for ourselves, anyway," Kenny said as Pascal went out. "I can't wait to go exploring tonight when we have our sleepover!"

*   *   *

The first morning of our visit to Paris was really cool! After breakfast we all piled on to the minibus, and Mrs Jackson drove us down to the River Seine, where we went on a boat trip. The boat took us along the river, past some of the most famous buildings in Paris. We saw the big cathedral, Notre Dame, which stands on an island in the middle of the river. The guide told us that Paris had started out there as a very small town. Then we saw the Louvre and the Musée D'Orsay, which are two really famous museums, and loads of other interesting things. Then, right at the end, we came to what we had all been waiting for.

"The Eiffel Tower!" Fliss squealed excitedly as we all stared at the Tower stretching right up to the sky.

"It's huge!" I gasped, craning my neck back. It was so tall, it was difficult to see it all in one go.

"We can go up it, can't we, Mrs Weaver?" Kenny asked eagerly as we climbed off the boat. "The guide said that we can go right to the top!"

Mrs Weaver smiled. "Of course we can," she said. "You get a wonderful view of Paris from up there."

"I can't wait!" Kenny said eagerly, and the rest of us nodded. Then Kenny nudged me. "Look at the Queen and the Goblin!" she whispered.

Emma and Emily were staring up at the Eiffel Tower, and looking a bit sick. I guess neither of them was very keen on heights!

"How high is the Eiffel Tower, Mrs Weaver?" Kenny asked innocently. "I didn't hear what the guide said."

"Oh, well, let me see." Mrs Weaver took out her guidebook. "The Tower is 300.51 metres tall."

Emily whispered something to Emma.

"Oh, and this is interesting," Mrs Weaver went on. "If the wind's very strong, apparently the Tower sways from side to side!"

The M&Ms looked up anxiously at the sky, and the Sleepover Club started to giggle.

"If anyone doesn't want to go up the Tower," Mrs Weaver called as she ushered us across the square to join the queue at the entrance, "they can wait down here with Mr Tate."

"So are you going to wimp out, Emma?" Frankie asked scornfully. "Or are you coming up the Eiffel Tower with the rest of us?"

"Of course we are!" Emma retorted haughtily, but her voice was a bit wobbly. I guess she didn't want to look like a coward in front of us, but she was as white as a ghost!

"Actually I might wait down here," Emily began timidly, but she soon shut up as the Queen gave her one of her snooty looks.

"Never mind, Emily," I said. "You and Emma can hang on to each other if it gets a bit windy!"

"Ha ha, very funny!" snapped Emma, pushing into the queue ahead of us.

"The Tower won't really sway about if it gets windy, will it?" Fliss asked nervously.

"Nah, don't worry about it," said Kenny, but Fliss didn't look too convinced.

"Mrs Weaver wouldn't let us go up there if it was dangerous, Fliss," I said. "Would she, Frankie?"

Frankie wasn't listening. "Hey, look over there!" she exclaimed. "Somebody's filming something!"

Immediately we all looked over to where Frankie was pointing, our eyes out on stalks. Sure enough, there was a large group of people in the square, and some of them were holding TV cameras.

"Maybe it's a news story," Fliss suggested.

"Yeah, maybe they've come to film the Eiffel Tower blowing around in the wind!" Kenny suggested wickedly.

"Oh, shut up, Kenny!" Fliss wailed, giving her a shove.

"No, hang on a minute! Look! It's them! It's her!" Lyndz could hardly get the words out because she was suddenly so excited. "It's *Westwood Street*!"

"*What!*" I gasped.

Westwood Street was our absolute *favourite* soap back home. It was set in a street in the middle of London, and we never, *ever* missed a single episode. In fact, we'd all asked our mums to tape it while we were away! Our most favourite actor was Danni Hart. She played a teenager called Billie Johnson who was always getting into trouble – a bit like the Sleepover Club, I guess!

"She's right!" Frankie spluttered. "There's Danni Hart!" And our eyes nearly popped out as we recognised the actress with her familiar cropped blonde hair. She was wearing a black leather jacket, and she was chatting to some of the other actors, who also looked familiar.

"That's Whatsisname – Chris Hamilton!" Fliss stuttered.

"And Liam Darcy!" Kenny added. "They must be filming some scenes for *Westwood Street* in Paris! Cool or what!"

By now the rest of the kids from our school had sussed what was going on, and the M&Ms looked as if they were about to wet themselves with excitement. None of the other tourists in the queue looked that bothered though. I guess they didn't get *Westwood Street* in Japan!

"Right, let's try that scene again," we

heard a man shout. He must have been the director or something.

"I'm not ready yet," Danni Hart called back with a frown.

The queue moved on a bit, and even though we were dying to go up the Tower, we didn't really want to move. We wanted to watch the filming.

"I wish I could get Danni Hart's autograph!" Fliss sighed as we shuffled forward reluctantly.

"I could get it for you!" Kenny boasted.

"Oh, behave, Kenny!" Frankie said with a grin. "Don't be so daft!"

Kenny stuck her tongue out at her. "Who's being daft? I *could* get it!"

"How?" Fliss asked. "We're about to go up the Eiffel Tower!"

"And Mrs Weaver won't let you," I added at the same time.

Kenny shrugged. "So what? I bet I can do it!"

"Go on, then!" Fliss said teasingly. "I *dare* you!"

At that moment Emma Hughes turned

round, and gave Kenny a smug grin. "I dare you too!" she said smoothly.

Well, you know what Kenny's like. The word *dare* to Kenny is like a red rag to a bull!

"Right, you're on!" Kenny snapped.

CHAPTER FOUR

"OK!" Emma agreed immediately while the rest of us looked at us each other in alarm. We'd only been winding Kenny up about the autograph – she didn't have a chance of getting it with Mrs Weaver in full view! And anyway, the actors were in the middle of filming – there was no way they'd stop to give autographs.

"Fine!" Kenny retorted airily.

"Kenny, this isn't a good idea!" Frankie warned her.

"It's a stupid idea!" Fliss added.

"Yeah, don't take the bet!" Lyndz and I said together.

"Too late, she already did!" the Queen pointed out smugly. Then she turned to Kenny and raised her eyebrows. "Unless you want to pull out of it, of course?"

"No way!" Kenny said firmly, and she glared at the rest of us. "It'll be cool – you'll see!"

We didn't think it would be cool at all, but we kept quiet because Kenny's our mate and we had to stand by her.

"Right, let's sort out the details," Emma said, grinning all over her face. "You're going to get Danni Hart's autograph for me. And if you don't, you're going to give me all the Leicester City autographs that you collected last season!"

We all gasped, and even Kenny did a bit of a double-take then. She'd spent *ages* getting every single one of the players' signatures. She was dead proud of them too. And the Queen knew it.

"What do you want with those autographs?"

Frankie said indignantly. "You don't even like football!"

Emma shrugged. "That's not the point! Well, Kenny?"

"All right," Kenny snapped. "And if I *do* get it, you and Emily have to be our slaves for the rest of the holiday! What do you say?"

"No way!" Emily began gruffly, but the Queen gave her a dig in the ribs.

"Don't be so silly, Emily! There's no way we can lose!"

The Goblin didn't look very convinced, but the Queen shut her up, like she always did.

"Fine." Emma Hughes turned to Kenny with a smug smile. "Go and get the autograph, then!"

"I'm going!" Kenny stood on tiptoe and checked where Mrs Weaver was. She was in front of us in the queue, and she was reading the guidebook. She had her head bent over it, and wasn't looking round. Mrs Jackson was in front of her, and she was talking to some of the other kids. "You lot cover for me!"

"Hurry up, Kenny!" Fliss said nervously.

"It'll be easy-peasy!" Kenny declared confidently and slid out of the queue, while the rest of the Sleepover Club watched anxiously.

"That's what *she* thinks!" Emma grinned.

It was then that I noticed just what the Queen was grinning about. We'd been so excited about the filming before, that we hadn't noticed there were some people with walkie-talkies who were politely but firmly keeping passers-by away from the scene of the filming.

"Look!" I nudged Frankie. "Kenny's never going to get past them!"

"If anyone can, Kenny can!" Frankie retorted, but she didn't sound too hopeful either.

Kenny sidled across the square towards the filming. She was heading straight for Danni Hart. Unfortunately, she was just about a few hundred yards away when someone called, "Right, let's try that scene again," and the actors moved into position.

"She's blown it!" Lyndz hissed as we all moved closer to the entrance to the Tower. "She'll never get it now!"

But we could hardly believe what happened next! Kenny must've decided to try and get Danni's autograph quickly before the filming started and before the people with walkie-talkies noticed her. Anyway, she rushed forward, tripped over a cable and fell SPLAT! on the ground... *right* in front of Danni Hart.

Danni was so surprised, she jumped backwards and bumped into one of the crew, who was holding a plastic cup of coffee. It went everywhere!

"I'm soaked!" Danni Hart screamed, her face red with fury. "Look at my jacket!"

"Oh no! Poor Kenny!" Fliss gasped.

We all watched, horrified, except for the Queen and the Goblin. Of course, they were in fits and holding on to each other for support. Meanwhile, poor old Kenny was struggling to her feet, looking *completely* embarrassed.

"What on earth is this idiot playing at?" Danni yelled, glaring at Kenny. "Someone get her out of here!"

Suddenly something flashed past us like a bolt of lightning. Mrs Weaver was on the warpath!

"Laura McKenzie! Get over here this minute!"

Mrs Weaver raced over to the film crew, took Kenny by the arm and began apologising to everyone. We couldn't hear what she was saying though, because Danni Hart was still yelling. I was going off her fast. She didn't seem very nice at all!

"Looks like we've won, Emily!" Emma giggled triumphantly. "High five!"

"Oh, shut up!" Frankie snapped as the Queen and the Goblin slapped palms. "It's not over yet!"

But it was. A grim-faced Mrs Weaver was marching a sheepish Kenny back over to the queue. "Stand here where I can keep an eye on you, Laura," she said in a freezing tone. "And if there's any more of this sort of behaviour, you'll spend tomorrow at the hotel writing lines!"

"Yeah, write 'I must not spill coffee over Danni Hart' a thousand times!" the Queen whispered to the Goblin, and they both sniggered.

"Are you OK, Kenny?" Lyndz whispered as Mrs Weaver stomped off to buy our tickets for the Tower.

"Yeah, I just feel like a prize prat!" Kenny groaned. "And Danni Hart was really gross – I don't even *want* her autograph now!"

"Yeah, she was a bit over the top, wasn't she?" I agreed.

"She went mad!" Kenny said, her face red with embarrassment. "I mean, it was only one tiny little cup of coffee!"

"Oh, Kenny," Emma called silkily. "I'll have those Leicester City autographs as soon as we get back home, then."

"Hang on just one little minute, Rat-Face!" Kenny glared at her. "I haven't given up yet!"

The Queen and the Goblin stared at her, and so did the Sleepover Club.

"What are you talking about?" Emma screeched. "You didn't get the autograph, so we win!"

"Yeah, but I still might." Kenny looked even more determined. "I heard some of the crew talking, and it turns out they're going to be filming in some more of the tourist places in Paris. So we might see them again!"

"Oh, that's totally stupid!" Emily began indignantly. "We won the bet fair and square!"

But the Queen nudged her. "No, if Kenny wants to keep the bet going, that's cool," she said with an evil smile. "But there are a few more conditions. If you don't get it by the time we go home, I want those autographs, *and* your new Leicester City shirt!"

"Done!" Kenny snapped immediately.

Frankie, Lyndz, Fliss and I groaned. Kenny was getting in deeper by the minute! But then I had a brilliant idea. It was obvious! We could forge Danni Hart's signature! Emma would never know…

"And don't even *think* about forging Danni Hart's signature!" the Queen went on. "We want to see you get the autograph in person – or it has to be on an official *Westwood Street* publicity photo!"

Kenny nodded airily. "You're gonna lose this one, Emma!" she said confidently as Mrs Weaver ushered us into the Tower.

"Kenny, are you *crazy*?" Frankie hissed as we began to climb the stairs. "You've played right into Emma's hands!"

"Yeah, Mrs Weaver won't let you go within a hundred metres of the filming!" Fliss pointed out. "Even if we *do* see them again!"

"And the film crew won't let you get near Danni Hart either," Lyndz added.

"And Danni Hart will probably run off if she sees you coming," I said.

"Oh, shut up, you lot!" Kenny snapped. "I'm not going to let Emma Hughes get one over on me. It'll be fine!"

Then she looked down and gasped. "Hey, look at this – we can see right down to the ground!"

It was a pretty weird experience going up the Eiffel Tower. The staircases were wide and sturdy, but you weren't *inside* anything – only within the open framework of the Tower. We went up to the highest floor in a lift, and the view was awesome! Even Mrs Weaver stopped looking grim, and started to have a good time. Then we went down to the lower floors to look at the shops. There was a Post Office too, and we all sent postcards of the Tower home to our mums and dads. Frankie even sent one to her baby sister Isobel, even though Izzy's only three months old!

"That was fantastic!" Lyndz sighed as we all headed back to the hotel, clutching our souvenirs.

"I hope my mum likes this," I said, looking at the miniature model of the Eiffel Tower I'd bought.

"I've got some French chocolate for our sleepover tonight," Fliss then announced, showing us an outsized bar.

"Excellent!" Frankie said. "Let's see what we can get tonight when we have dinner."

"We could nick some French bread and

some cheese and butter," Lyndz suggested. "What d'you think, Kenny?"

"Huh?" Kenny was deep in thought. "Yeah. Fine. Whatever."

"You're worrying about getting that autograph, aren't you?" Frankie said as we went into the hotel.

"Nah, 'course not!" But we could tell Kenny was just putting a brave face on it. "I'll get it, no problem."

"Yeah, 'course you will!" we all agreed, but we couldn't help pulling faces at each other behind Kenny's back. It wasn't going to be easy…

But when we went upstairs to our room, we had something else to worry about. As Frankie unlocked the door, she gave a little scream.

"What's that?"

"What's what?" we chorused, all trying to push our way into the room at once. But Frankie got in first, and rushed over to her bed. There was a piece of paper lying on her pillow. It was a note.

Vive le Sleepover Club!

"Help!" the note read.
"I am being kept a prisoner in the attic!"

CHAPTER FIVE

We all stood there staring at the note for about two minutes in silence, our eyes nearly dropping out of our heads. We could hardly believe what we were reading.

"It can't be real!" Lyndz said at last. "It must be a joke!"

"But who wrote it?" Frankie asked, frowning at the piece of paper.

"Oh, it's obvious, isn't it?" Kenny snorted. "It must be the M&Ms!"

Fliss was shaking her head. "No, it couldn't have been. The note wasn't here when we went out this morning and locked the door."

"And we've been out all day and so have they," Lyndz pointed out.

"Yeah, there's no way it could have been them," I agreed.

"It must be real then!" Fliss gasped. "Who do you think is up there?"

We all stared fearfully up at the bedroom ceiling as if we were expecting someone to drop through it like Father Christmas! It was weird to think of someone being held prisoner right over our heads.

"I told you I heard something up in the attic last night!" Frankie reminded us breathlessly. "It must have been that person, whoever it is!"

"I bet it's something to do with that spooky maid, Chantal." Fliss shuddered. "She looks like something out of a horror film – maybe she's a witch!"

"Or a vampire," Kenny suggested, baring her teeth. "And the attic's where she keeps her victims! We've got to go and find out."

"But we're not allowed up those stairs," I reminded her.

"Oh, knickers to that!" Kenny snorted. "Of course they don't want anyone going up there if they're keeping someone prisoner! But that's not going to stop us, is it?"

"Well, actually..." Fliss began, looking absolutely terrified, but she stopped when Kenny glared at her.

"Look, if we wait till everyone's asleep, we'll be fine," Kenny said urgently. "Someone could be in real trouble up there."

We all looked up at the ceiling again. Kenny was right. If someone was in trouble we had to try and help

"Come on, let's go down and get something to eat." Kenny went over to the door. "We can't do anything till tonight, and I'm starving!"

Frankie hid the note under her pillow just in case Scary Chantal came in, and we all went down to the dining room. The M&Ms were already in there, and they started giggling and whispering about us as we walked in. They obviously thought Kenny had no hope of getting Danni Hart's signature, and they were looking forward to making Kenny keep her part of the bargain when we got home.

"Hey, Kenny!" called Ryan Scott, who's in our class. As we went past his table, he stuck out his foot, trying to trip one of us up. We all glared at him, except Fliss who giggled. She's had a bit of a thing about Ryan Scott for ages. "Did you enjoy your *trip* today?"

Then he and his best mate Danny McCloud roared with laughter, and the stupid M&Ms joined in. So did all the other kids from our school.

"Oh, ha ha, very funny," Kenny said shortly.

"Yeah, I thought so!" Ryan spluttered.

"Bet Danni Hart didn't though!" Danny McCloud pointed out, and everyone laughed even harder.

"I've got to get that autograph!" Kenny said grimly as we sat down at our table looking gloomy. "If the M&Ms get one over on us, we'll never hear the end of it."

"Oh, let's forget about the M&Ms!" I said. "I want to enjoy our sleepover tonight."

The thought of the sleepover cheered us all up a bit. While we ate our dinner, we talked about what we were going to do that evening. We were also busy squirrelling away bits of bread and cheese to have later at our midnight feast. Mrs Weaver was sitting quite near us, so it was a good laugh trying not to let her see us stuffing bits of French bread into our pockets!

The hotel had a big games room, and after dinner we all piled in there to play table tennis and watch TV. We couldn't really understand much of the TV though, because it was all in French! Anyway, we were only filling in time before our sleepover, so when the teachers came to round us all up for bed, we were quite pleased. At least it meant we got the M&Ms out of our hair.

"I can't *wait* to find out who's in the attic," Kenny muttered as we went upstairs to our room. "Maybe we can help them to escape!"

"If we do find someone, I think we should tell Mrs Weaver," said Fliss firmly. "'Specially if that Chantal's got anything to do with it!"

"Yeah, yeah, 'course we will," Kenny assured her. "I reckon Mrs Weaver can sort Chantal out, no problem!"

"Ssh! Someone's coming down the stairs!" I hissed.

We turned the corner and came face to face with Pascal. He nodded and smiled politely at us.

"*Bon soir, bon soir*," he said.

We all looked at each other blankly.

"I think that means goodnight," Frankie said with a frown.

"*Bon soir*, Pascal!" we all chorused, and he looked quite impressed!

"Hey, Pascal, come with me." And Kenny suddenly grabbed Pascal's arm and started pulling him up the stairs.

"Kenny, what are you doing?" I asked as we all chased after them. Pascal looked a bit bewildered to say the least.

"I just want to show him the staircase to

the attic," Kenny called back over her shoulder. "He might be able to help us!"

"Kenny, he doesn't even speak English!" Frankie grumbled. But Kenny ignored her. She took Pascal to the bottom of the staircase outside our room, and pointed upwards.

"What is up there?" she asked slowly.

Pascal stared at us. He looked really scared all of a sudden. Then he shook his head, gabbled something in French and dashed down the stairs, nearly falling over himself in his hurry to get away.

"What's up with him?" Fliss said in a quavery voice. "He looked really frightened!"

"That settles it!" Kenny said, sounding very determined. "There is *definitely* something weird about that attic – and we're going to find out what. Tonight!"

"*Bonjour*, everyone, and welcome to our French sleepover!" Frankie announced, bouncing up and down on her bed in her bright purple pyjamas. "*Ça sent très mauvais ici!*"

"What does that mean?" Kenny asked as we all looked impressed.

"I read it in my phrasebook." Frankie grinned. "I think it means 'I hope you all have a very good time'!"

"No, it doesn't, Frankie, you fibber!" Lyndz announced after flipping through the phrasebook. "It means 'There is a very bad smell in here'!"

"Oh, well, I must have got it wrong!" Frankie yawned. We all attacked her with our pillows, and ended up in a tangled heap on her bed.

"What shall we do now?" Fliss asked.

"Let's have our midnight feast," Lyndz suggested.

"We could write our diaries," I said.

"Nah, let's do the Can-Can!" Kenny grinned.

We all thought that was a great idea, so we stood in a line between the beds and linked arms.

"OK, right leg first!" Kenny instructed us as we began high-kicking into the air. "No, *right* leg, Fliss, you dummy!"

We all tried to hum the Can-Can tune as we kicked our legs up, but we were giggling so much we were nearly choking. Then Lyndz tried to kick her leg a bit too high. She overbalanced and fell back on to the bed, pulling the rest of us with her.

"I think we need a bit more practice!" she spluttered. "Hic!"

"No hiccups allowed!" Kenny thumped Lyndz on the back.

"Yeah, if you hiccup, you've got to do it in French!" Frankie added. Lyndz started laughing and that seemed to cure her!

"Can-Can dancers do the splits as well," said Fliss. "Can anyone do them?"

We spent about ten minutes all trying to do the splits, but it was pretty hopeless. Then Frankie managed the splits after all – she split her pyjama trousers right along the middle! The rest of us nearly died laughing. Finally we had our midnight feast, and we scoffed all of Fliss's chocolate and all of the bread and cheese.

"What shall we do now?" I asked.

"Ssh!" Kenny hissed as she snaffled the last square of chocolate. "Listen!"

We all listened hard.

"What is it?" Fliss asked fearfully. "I can't hear anything."

"Neither can I!" Kenny grinned at us. "Which means that everyone's asleep. So come on!" She bounced off her bed, and grabbed her torch from her bag. "Let's go and explore the attic!"

We all climbed off our beds, and followed Kenny over to the door. My heart was thumping hard. I think everyone else's was too, by the looks on their faces.

"I'm not going first," Fliss said in a shaky voice. "Or last."

"I'll go first," Kenny said bravely. "Follow me!"

We all tiptoed out of our bedroom door – Kenny first, followed by me, Lyndz, Fliss and then Frankie. We looked up. Above us, the old dusty staircase wound out of sight into the darkness.

"Maybe we should just tell Mrs Weaver about the note," Fliss suggested weakly as

Kenny put her foot on the first step. It creaked like mad.

"SSSHHHH!" the rest of us hissed.

"OK, don't panic!" Kenny whispered back. She put her foot on the second step, and it creaked like a door opening in a horror movie.

Then we all froze in terror as we heard another noise. Footsteps were coming swiftly up the stairs behind us which led to our room. We could see a long, thin shadow on the wall, getting closer and closer... Someone was coming! We were so shocked we couldn't even nip back into our bedroom.

"Quick!" Kenny gabbled, trying to rush down the stairs and only succeeding in bumping into the rest of us. "Let's get out of here!"

But it was too late.

"*Qu'est-ce que vous faites là, exactement?*" said a loud, angry voice.

CHAPTER SIX

Chantal the scary maid was standing there, glaring at us, hands on her hips. We were all rooted to the spot.

"*Où allez-vous?*" Chantal snapped angrily. "*Retournez à votre chambre immédiatement!*"

We couldn't understand what she was saying, but we could tell by the look on her face that she wasn't offering us a nice cup of tea! We all scurried down the stairs and back into our bedroom. Chantal stood in the doorway with her arms folded, glaring at us as we scrambled into bed. She didn't move until we were all under our duvets. Then she sniffed loudly and turned off the light, closing the door behind her.

"Whew! That old battle-axe definitely does not want us looking in the attic!" Kenny bounced out of bed and rushed over to switch the light back on. "Why do you think *that* is?"

"It's probably where she keeps her broomstick!" I said with a grin.

"Ssh, she might be listening outside the door!" Fliss shivered. "I nearly died when she came round the corner!"

"She must know that there's someone being kept prisoner up there," I pointed out. "That's why she was so mad."

"What are we going to do?" Lyndz asked. "If there *is* someone being kept prisoner in the attic, we can't just leave them there."

"We'll have to give it another go," Frankie decided. "Tomorrow night. Chantal can't possibly watch us the *whole* time."

"Cool!" said Kenny. "We'll show Chantal she can't mess with the Sleepover Club and get away with it!"

*   *   *

I was the first one awake the next morning. I sat up in bed yawning and rubbing my eyes. Everyone was still flat out, and Fliss and Lyndz were snoring a bit.

I pushed back the duvet and swung my legs out of bed. Then I stopped. I'd just noticed something. There was a piece of paper lying on the floor. Someone had pushed another message under our door in the middle of the night!

"Hey, wake up you lot!" I yelled as I dived across the room and grabbed the piece of paper.

"Urgh!" Kenny mumbled, pushing the duvet off her head and sitting up.

"Oh, shut up, Rosie!" Frankie yawned.

"It's not time to get up, is it?" Fliss moaned.

"That cheese has given me a stomach-ache!" Lyndz groaned.

"Be quiet, you lot!" I gabbled, as I read the note through quickly. "The prisoner in the attic has sent us another note!"

That got them all going!

"*What!*" Kenny and Lyndz both jumped

out of bed and collided slap-bang with Frankie and Fliss who were already charging across the room towards me.

"Yeah, she pushed it under our door last night while we were asleep!" I waved the piece of paper at them.

"*She?*" Lyndz repeated, "Who is it then?"

"Listen!" I read the note aloud. "Hello, my friends. My name is Jeanne. I am a prisoner in the attic, and I am only set free during the day when everyone is out and at night time when everyone is asleep. I have to do all the cooking and cleaning round here. Come to the attic tonight at midnight. Please help me – you are my only hope!"

We all stared at each other in amazement.

"We've got to help her!" I said.

"We will," Kenny said firmly. "We can't let that horrible Chantal get away with this!"

"Maybe we should take the note to Mrs Weaver," Fliss suggested for the third time.

"Fliss could be right," Frankie agreed solemnly. "This is getting pretty serious!"

"Mm, but we ought to check it out first,"

Kenny insisted. "We'll look pretty stupid if it turns out to be a fake!"

"Kenny's right," Lyndz said. "And we're not exactly Mrs Weaver's favourite pupils at the moment either…"

"I don't think it *is* a fake." Frankie studied the note carefully.

Kenny nodded. "Neither do I. Look, all we've got to do is check it out first. If it's true, then we'll have to let the teachers know."

"OK," we all agreed.

"What are we going to do then?" Fliss asked, her teeth chattering.

"We'll go up to the attic again tonight," Kenny said grimly. "And this time nothing's going to stop us. Not even Scary Chantal…"

We were all feeling pretty fired up about going to the attic to rescue Jeanne that night, so we were a bit rowdy at breakfast. It wasn't until Mrs Weaver gave us the evil eye a few times that we calmed down! Anyway, there wasn't anything we could do until the evening, so we just tried to enjoy ourselves and forget about it for a bit.

Until the M&Ms came in and sat down at the table next to us, that is.

"I wonder where the *Westwood Street* actors will be filming today," the Queen remarked in a loud voice as she nibbled a croissant.

"Miles away from wherever we are, I hope!" the Goblin said gruffly, and they both roared with laughter as if Emily had just made the joke of the century.

Kenny groaned, and buried her nose in her glass of orange juice.

"I'd almost forgotten about the bet, what with all that stuff last night!" she said. "Remember, you lot, we've got to keep our eyes open for the film crew!"

We all nodded.

After breakfast everyone piled into the minibus again for another day's sightseeing. Mr Tate drove us to Montmartre, which is a really pretty part of Paris. It had lots of little streets, and a big white church called Sacre-

Cœur, which we were allowed to go into and look around. We were allowed to go shopping too, and we bought loads of souvenirs and postcards. Then we all got back on the minibus, and we were taken to the most famous museum in Paris, the Louvre. It was so big that we were only going round bits of it.

"Right, you'll all recognise this famous picture," Mrs Weaver announced as she led us into one of the rooms. We couldn't see much though, because there was a big crowd of tourists round the famous picture, whatever it was.

"I can see it!" Frankie announced excitedly. She's a right beanpole, so she could just about see what was hanging on the wall if she stood on her toes. She looked over the heads of a big crowd of Japanese tourists. "It's the Mona Lisa!"

"Well done, Frankie," said Mrs Weaver approvingly. "Yes, it is the Mona Lisa."

"What's Lisa moaning about now?" Kenny giggled, nudging me in the ribs.

"Oh, very funny!" I nudged her back as

some of the other tourists moved away and we managed to edge our way forward. "But you're right – she doesn't look very happy, does she?"

We looked at some of the other stuff in the museum, including a statue of a lady with no arms that Mrs Weaver said was the Venus de Milo. Then we were taken into a park to eat the packed lunches the hotel had prepared for us. We were starving, so we all got stuck in. All except Fliss, who started opening her sandwiches and peering into them as if she expected to find a slug or something!

"What *are* you doing, Flissy?" Kenny asked in amazement.

Fliss looked nervous. "What if it was Chantal who made the sandwiches?"

"What if it was?" Frankie asked, looking puzzled.

Fliss looked around, and lowered her voice. "Well, she might be trying to poison us!"

"Don't be daft, Fliss!" said Frankie. Lyndz and I giggled, but Kenny frowned.

"You could be right, Fliss! Come to think if

it, I'm feeling a bit funny – urgh!" Kenny clutched her throat and fell over backwards, sprawling out motionless on the grass. Fliss squealed, and the rest of us howled with laughter.

"Oh, very clever!" Fliss poked Kenny in the stomach, and Kenny sat up, laughing her head off.

"No sign of the film crew yet today," remarked Emma Hughes smugly as she and Emily Berryman went past us. "Looks like you won't be getting that autograph after all, Kenny."

Kenny stopped laughing and stuck her tongue out at the Queen's back. "The Queen's right, for once," she said gloomily. "I just hope we catch up with the filming again soon…"

Guess what? We did! After lunch we went to see the famous cathedral, Notre Dame. We'd seen it from the boat the day before, but now we had a chance to look at it properly, and go inside. It was a really big, impressive building with lots of funny gargoyles and other carvings on the front. But the very first thing we noticed was that the film crew were there again, along with the actors Danni Hart and Liam Darcy. And they were shooting a scene outside the cathedral!

"Cool!" Kenny exclaimed in delight. She pulled a face at the Queen and the Goblin, who'd also spotted the film crew and were looking like thunder. "This is where I really rub Emma's nose in it!"

"Kenny, I don't think you should be the one who gets the autograph," Frankie said firmly as Mrs Weaver and the other teachers ushered us over to the cathedral entrance, keeping us away from the filming.

"What?" Kenny said with a frown. "Why not?"

"If Mrs Weaver catches you, you're dead," Frankie explained. "And if Danni Hart recognises you, you're dead too."

"Frankie's right," I chimed in. "One of us had better do it."

"No way!" Kenny said crossly. "It's *my* bet!"

Just then Mrs Weaver looked round and fixed Kenny with a grim stare. "Laura, I don't want to see you going anywhere near that film crew today. Are you listening to me?"

"Yes, Mrs Weaver," Kenny muttered.

"See?" we all chorused.

Kenny shrugged. "Weaver wouldn't see me if I—"

"Do you really want to miss the trip to Disneyland and stay in the hotel all day writing lines?" Fliss interrupted her in a severe voice.

Kenny pulled a face. "No."

"OK, then, Rosie and I will do it." Frankie looked at Lyndz and Fliss. "Take Kenny into the cathedral, and don't let her out of your sight!"

"Come on, Kenny!" said Lyndz. She and Fliss each took one of Kenny's arms and dragged her off. Kenny went very reluctantly, but she went. Most of the others had already gone inside, except for Mr Tate who was rounding up the stragglers, and the M&Ms, who were obviously hanging around to see what was going to happen.

"So you've chickened out, have you, McKenzie!" Emma Hughes gloated as Kenny, Fliss and Lyndz went past them into the cathedral. "I knew you didn't have the nerve!"

"I haven't chickened out!" Kenny retorted. "Frankie and Rosie are going to get the autograph!"

The Queen looked superior. "That wasn't the bet – the bet was that *you* were to get it! That means you've lost!"

"No way!" Kenny retorted. "Do you want this autograph or not?"

We all looked at the Queen, who was obviously thinking about what she was going to do. In a way, she was right. She *had* made the bet with Kenny, so we were breaking the conditions. But I could easily tell what Emma Hughes was thinking. She was thinking that this was a great chance to get some of the rest of the Sleepover Club into trouble, *and* still win the bet!

"All right," Emma Hughes said at last.

"So you agree that Frankie and Rosie can get the autograph?" Kenny asked.

Vive le Sleepover Club!

The Queen and the Goblin both nodded. Then they turned round and grinned evilly at me and Frankie. "This I've got to see!" said Emma Hughes smugly.

CHAPTER SEVEN

"Come on, Rosie." Frankie gave me a nudge, and we slipped away from everyone else.

"Did you see that smug smile on the Queen's face?" I muttered. "She really thinks that we're going to mess this up!"

"I know," Frankie replied. "And this could be our last chance, so we've got to get it right!"

Frankie and I quickly scurried out of sight behind a big group of Japanese tourists so that we could check out the lie of the land. Mr Tate was still trying to get everyone inside the cathedral, but he hadn't noticed us. He was too busy sorting out an argument between Ryan Scott and Danny McCloud. Meanwhile, Danni Hart and Liam Darcy, who played her boyfriend in the soap, were walking along in front of the cathedral hand in hand, being filmed. Then they stopped to kiss and hug each other.

"OK, cut!" shouted someone. "That's a wrap. Well done, everyone."

As Frankie and I watched closely, Danni Hart began to complain about something. We couldn't hear what she was saying, but we could tell she wasn't happy. She was waving her arms about and looking really mad.

"I don't like her one bit now!" Frankie whispered to me.

"I know, she's a right pain in the behind!" I whispered back. "Do you think she'll give us her autograph?"

It didn't look too hopeful. Danni Hart was red in the face and looked as if she was going to explode any minute!

"We've got to try," Frankie said. "Come on!"

We were about to go over to the film crew when it happened. All of a sudden we were surrounded by a big crowd of Japanese tourists, all smiling and holding their cameras out to us and talking in Japanese. We were so hemmed in, we couldn't move.

"What are they saying?" I asked Frankie nervously.

"How should I know?" Frankie gasped. "I don't speak Japanese!"

Just then one of the women shoved her camera into Frankie's hands and pointed at the cathedral and then at herself.

"Oh, I think she wants me to take her photo!" Frankie said with a grin.

"Hurry up then!" I said urgently. "We've got to get that autograph!"

Then an old man shoved a camera at me too, so I took his picture standing outside the cathedral while Frankie was taking the woman's. Then all of a sudden, *another* tourist was pushing a camera into my hand!

"No, I can't!" I said helplessly.

But it was no good. They didn't understand

what we were saying! Frankie was in the same mess too. As fast as we snapped one person, another camera was pushed straight into our hands. We must have taken about thirty photos!

Then suddenly Frankie let out a wail. "Oh no!"

I looked up just in time to see Danni Hart and Liam Darcy get into a big black car and speed off. The filming had finished.

"We've missed them!" I groaned. "Oh, rats!"

"Frankie! Rosie!" called Mr Tate impatiently from the cathedral entrance. "I'm waiting for you to come inside, please!"

Frankie and I managed to get away from the Japanese tourists, and we went gloomily over to Mr Tate.

"Well done, girls," he said. "That was very kind of you, taking all those photos."

Frankie and I just looked at each other as he ushered us inside the cathedral. Yes, the tourists had got all their photos all right – but we'd missed getting that precious autograph!

The cathedral was beautiful inside, but we weren't really in the mood to appreciate it. We looked around for the others, and spotted them at the same time as they saw us.

"Well?" Kenny, Fliss and Lyndz came over as fast as they could without actually running. We *were* in a church, after all! "Did you get it?"

Wearily Frankie and I shook our heads.

"No!" Kenny exclaimed in horror.

"We got ambushed by a gang of Japanese tourists who wanted us to take their pictures," Frankie explained.

"And by the time we got away, the filming had finished," I added gloomily.

Suddenly there was a muffled snort from behind us. We turned round to see the Queen and the Goblin stuffing their hands in their mouths to stop themselves from laughing.

"Oh, shut up!" Kenny hissed. "The bet's not over yet!"

"Only two more days to go!" Emily Berryman said gloatingly. "And you might not see the film crew again anyway!"

"We will!" Kenny said firmly, but we could tell that she was getting a bit depressed about it. I mean, for all we knew, filming in Paris could have finished and Danni Hart might be heading back to England right at this very minute!

"Yeah, we would have got the autograph today for sure if it hadn't been for all those tourists wanting their picture taken!" I said, to back Kenny up.

Emma and Emily almost turned purple trying not to laugh. Suddenly I got very suspicious.

"Did you two tell those tourists that Frankie and I would take their pictures?" I asked furiously.

"Now why would we do a thing like that?" the Queen asked airily, and she and Emily sauntered off, smirking.

"They *did*!" I said. "It was all their fault!"

"Well, it's too late to worry about that now," Frankie said solemnly. "Let's just hope we see the film crew again before the holiday's over..."

*   *   *

"Quiet!" Frankie ordered us as we all tiptoed over to the bedroom door. It was five minutes to midnight, and we were on our way to rescue Jeanne! "Don't make a sound. Don't even breathe! We don't want Chantal to catch us again like she did last night!"

"I'm scared!" Fliss moaned as Frankie opened the door.

"Oh, don't worry, Fliss!" Kenny said confidently. "There's five of us and only one of Chantal!"

"Yeah, but if she's a vampire, she'll have magic powers!" Fliss muttered, unconvinced.

"Never mind, I'll sort her out, just like *Buffy the Vampire Slayer*!" Kenny grinned, and pretended to karate-kick the door. Her foot hit the handle, and we all nearly died.

"QUIET, Kenny!" Frankie hissed. "Or you can stay behind!"

"Yeah, maybe we shouldn't all go anyway," Fliss said eagerly. "It'd be much quieter if only *one* person went."

"Does anyone want to go on their own?"

Frankie asked, peering round the door up the dark staircase. It looked even more scary than the night before!

We all glanced at each other. Even Kenny didn't look too keen.

"OK, we all go then!" said Frankie firmly. "Is that all right with everyone?"

We all nodded, and followed her out of the room. Kenny, who was last, pulled the door shut with a gentle click.

"Just in case Chantal comes nosing around!" she said.

"Right, don't step in the middle of the first two stairs," Frankie instructed us as she switched on her torch. "They creak, remember?"

We all linked hands, and set off up the stairs as quietly and quickly as we could. All we had to do was get to the curve in the staircase, and then we'd be round the corner and out of sight from our landing. We'd feel a lot safer then. It was only about fourteen steps to get there, but it seemed to take us hours. At last Kenny followed the rest of us round the corner and we all slumped against the wall and breathed a sigh of relief.

"OK, we'd still better be quiet," Frankie said in a low voice, as she played the beam of her torch up the stairs ahead of her. "Chantal might be up in the attic with Jeanne, for all we know!"

"Hold on," I whispered. "What are we going to do if she is?"

We all looked at each other. "I told you, I'll do my *Buffy* act!" Kenny said, but that didn't make any of us feel much better.

"Maybe we should just all rush in at once," Lyndz suggested. "She can't catch all of us at the same time!"

Fliss gave a little squeal. "I'll die if she catches me!"

But we'd gone too far to turn back now! We carried on up the stairs for a little way. Then the staircase ended, and we came out on to a dark, narrow landing. There was only one door up there – a big, thick, wooden one. A large, old-fashioned key hung on a rusty nail on the wall beside the door.

"This is it!" Kenny whispered. "This must be the attic!"

My heart was thumping and I was shivering, even though it wasn't cold. Fliss looked absolutely petrified, Frankie was pale, Lyndz's eyes were as big as dinner plates and even Kenny was shaking a bit.

Kenny reached out for the key, but Frankie grabbed her arm. "Let's knock on the door first," she suggested.

"No!" Fliss moaned. "What if Chantal's in there?"

"We'll have to take the chance!" Frankie said. "We don't want to alarm Jeanne."

Kenny nodded. Taking a deep breath, she tapped gently on the door.

"Jeanne?" she hissed. "Jeanne, it's us – the girls from downstairs. The ones you sent the note to. We've come to rescue you!"

No answer.

"Turn the torch off, Frankie!" Kenny hissed. "We're going in!"

"Why do we have to turn the torch off?" Fliss groaned.

"Because if Chantal's in there, we don't want her to see us!" Kenny explained. "And we can make a better getaway in the dark!"

Frankie obediently switched the torch off, and we all gasped. It was so dark up there that we couldn't see our hands in front of our faces.

"If we have to run for it, we're all going to fall down the stairs and break our necks!" Lyndz whispered. I don't think she was joking either!

"Right, here we go!" Kenny grabbed the key off the hook, and put it in the lock. It turned with a squeaking sound that grated on my ears. Kenny pushed the door, and it swung open with a loud CRE-E-E-AK! It was *just* like a horror film – but it was more scary that any horror film I've ever seen!

We all peered over Kenny's shoulder, but we couldn't see a thing. The room was in pitch darkness, just like the landing.

"Jeanne?" Kenny called cautiously, but there was still no answer. She fumbled for the light switch but couldn't find it. "Put the torch on, Frankie."

Vive le Sleepover Club!

It was *then* that we heard it! A low, scary, spinechilling moan from inside the room! *"AAAAARRRRRGGGGH!"*

CHAPTER EIGHT

"Wha-wha-wha-what's that?" Kenny gasped. "Who's there?"

The rest of us were too petrified even to scream. We just stood there, clutching each other's hands. I don't know about the others, but it felt like my blood had frozen in my veins and I couldn't move a muscle!

Then, all of a sudden, we turned and rushed for the stairs. There was a clatter as Frankie dropped her torch in the mad panic, but we didn't stop. We all hurtled down the staircase and back to our bedroom, panting hard. It was a wonder none of us tripped and hurt ourselves, we moved so fast! I was last into the room, and I slammed the door and locked and bolted it.

"What – what – what – what was *that*?" Fliss gabbled, her hair almost standing up on end. "It was *horrible*!"

"It was the worst noise I've ever heard in my whole life!" Frankie gasped.

"D'you think Jeanne's a ghost?" Lyndz asked breathlessly.

"Maybe it was Chantal trying to scare us," Kenny suggested.

"Well, she did a great job!" I spluttered. "I'm terrified!"

We all flopped down on to the big double bed, and tried to get our breath back.

"It couldn't have been Chantal in there," Frankie said with a frown. "The door was locked and the key was on the hook. Whoever was in there was locked in."

"Then it must have been Jeanne." Kenny looked puzzled. "So why did she scare us away? She knew we were coming at midnight!"

It was a complete mystery. We all stared at each other nervously. What on earth were we going to do now?

"I still think we should—" Fliss began.

"Yeah, yeah, I know, tell Mrs Weaver!" Kenny finished the sentence off for her. "But do you reckon she'd believe us?"

"No, she wouldn't," Frankie said. "She'd think we were having her on!"

None of us had a clue what to do next. But for the moment, we had some other things to worry about.

"Ow!" Lyndz groaned. "I banged my ankle running down the stairs!"

"And I left my torch behind!" Frankie muttered.

We all looked at each other in horror.

"Now Chantal will know we've been up there!" I said in a trembly voice.

"No, she won't," Kenny said confidently. "She won't know that the torch is Frankie's."

"She might have seen it lying around when she cleaned our room," Fliss pointed out. We all stared at each other, dismayed.

"We'll have to take the chance," I said.

Frankie cleared her throat. "Actually, it's got my name written on it!" she admitted, and we all groaned.

"We'll have to get it back then," Lyndz said with a shiver. We all looked over at the locked and bolted door. None of us made a move.

"I think we should leave it till the morning," Kenny suggested, and we all nodded thankfully. We'd had enough excitement for one night!

We all climbed wearily into bed, and for once, we all left our bedside lights on. We didn't talk much, and we didn't sing our sleepover song. But it was a very long time before any of us got to sleep…

"Right, let's go!" Kenny said in a determined voice, stomping over to the door. It was morning, and we'd all got up for breakfast even though we hadn't had much sleep. "We're gonna get Frankie's torch back, and show Chantal that she doesn't scare us!"

It's a lot easier to be brave in daylight than it is in the dark! Even Fliss didn't look *too* scared as we marched over to the door behind Kenny.

"We're going to solve this mystery once and for all!" Kenny announced as she pulled the door open, "And then—"

She stopped. Frankie's torch was on the floor, standing neatly on its end just outside our door.

"My torch!" Frankie grabbed it. "Who put it there?"

"Maybe it just rolled down the stairs and landed outside our door," Fliss said hopefully.

"What, on its end?" Lyndz said. "Someone must have put it there!"

"Yes, but who?" I asked.

We all began feeling a bit jittery again, but Kenny made for the stairs. "Come on," she called over her shoulder. "There's something weird going on here!"

The staircase wasn't half as scary by daylight as it was at night, but I think we were all feeling rather nervous. I know *I* was! We went up to the attic door and stopped. The big key was back on the hook, and Kenny lifted it off, and inserted it in the keyhole.

"Someone must have put that back after we unlocked the door last night," Kenny said.

"Just hurry up and open the door!" Fliss said in a trembling voice.

"Right, get ready!" Kenny instructed us.

"What for?" I asked.

"I dunno." Kenny turned the key. "But be ready just in case!"

She pushed the door. It creaked open and we all craned our necks so that we could see into the room.

It was a large room. And it was stuffed with buckets, mops, dusters and cans of polish, plus lots of cardboard boxes filled with old clothes, old books and other junk. We all stared. We just couldn't believe our eyes.

"It's just a junk room!" Kenny said, dazed. "There's no prisoner here!"

"And it looks like Chantal keeps her cleaning stuff here too!" I added.

We all started shuffling our feet and feeling a bit stupid.

"Maybe we should look around in case all this is just a front," I suggested.

So we did. We got all dusty and dirty looking behind the boxes and checking out every corner of the room. But there was no-one being kept prisoner up there at all!

"Someone sent those notes, though!" Frankie frowned. "Who could it have been?"

"I don't know," Kenny said grimly. "But when I find out, they're dead!"

We locked the door up, and trailed down the stairs. We were beginning to feel *really* stupid by now!

"Thank goodness we didn't go to Mrs Weaver!" Fliss said. "I always said it was a bad idea!"

As we turned the corner of the stairs, we got a bit of a shock. Pascal was standing at the bottom by our bedroom door. He waved to us, and then began to laugh. In fact, he laughed so hard it looked like he was going to be sick!

"What's the matter with *him*?" Frankie asked, puzzled.

"Nothing is the matter," Pascal said. In perfect English! We all gasped. "I was wondering if you liked my little surprise last night!"

"You – you – you speak English!" Fliss spluttered.

"Yes." Pascal grinned. "I overhear you talking about going up to the attic on the day you arrived, so I think to play a little joke on you!"

We couldn't believe it.

"So you wrote those notes?" Kenny stammered.

Pascal nodded. "You played a joke on me, remember? You teach me some English?" We all turned pink. "So now I play a joke on you!"

"Well, I guess that's fair enough!" Kenny tried to keep a straight face, but then she began to laugh. "But you really had us going there for a while!"

Pascal looked pleased with himself. "Yes, I think it was a good joke too! A prisoner in the attic!"

We all started to laugh then. We'd been well and truly done, and it served us right! But I think we were all secretly relieved too.

"But how did you manage to lock yourself in the attic, and leave the key outside for us?" Frankie asked.

Pascal dived into his pocket and pulled out a key which was an exact copy of the one on the hook upstairs. "I have a spare!" he said triumphantly.

"We thought Chantal was the one who was keeping Jeanne prisoner!" I told him. "We're all a bit scared of her!"

"Oh, Chantal is OK," Pascal shrugged. "When you know her!"

"That was a really good joke, Pascal," Kenny said. "You and I should get together and talk about jokes sometime!"

We all groaned.

"You know, Pascal?" Kenny went on as we all clattered downstairs to breakfast. "If you have any more good ideas for jokes, you should play them on the M&Ms!"

"The M&Ms?" Pascal looked puzzled.

We explained about Emma Hughes and Emily Berryman. Pascal nodded. "Ah, yes, the snob girl and the one with the voice like a man!"

We all fell about laughing.

"That's them!" Kenny said. Then she turned to the rest of us. "We've just got to get that autograph today! Where are we going?"

"Mrs Weaver said we were visiting the Palace of Versailles," Lyndz said.

"Well, let's hope Danni Hart's there too, or I've only got tomorrow left to get that autograph!" Kenny muttered.

Pascal was looking confused, so Frankie filled him in on Kenny's bet with the M&Ms.

"Good luck!" he said with a grin as we went into the dining room. "*Bonne chance!*"

"What's that mean?" Fliss asked, and we all groaned.

"Good luck, of course!" Kenny said as we went over to our table.

"We're going to need it," I muttered as the Queen and the Goblin sauntered into the dining room, throwing incredibly smug looks in our direction.

"Only two days to go, Emily!" the Queen remarked as they passed our table.

"I know, they don't stand a chance!" the Goblin gloated happily.

"That's what they think!" Kenny muttered bravely, but the thought of losing the bet to the M&Ms almost put us off our croissants.

The Palace of Versailles was completely brilliant. In fact, the only thing that was wrong with the Palace of Versailles was that the *Westwood Street* film crew weren't there! So we couldn't do very much about getting Danni Hart's autograph. Mrs Weaver told us that the palace was built by a French king called King Louis the Fourteenth, whose nickname was the Sun King. He wanted it to be better and more beautiful than any other palace. And it was. It was really big, with loads of rooms full of paintings and gold furniture and huge crystal chandeliers. My favourite room was the Hall of Mirrors, where Mrs Weaver said the King and Queen would hold dances for all their courtiers. The gardens were amazing too, with enormous fountains and lakes.

Of course, Kenny managed to fall slap-bang right into the middle of one of the fountains! She had a bet with Frankie (yes, another bet!) that she could walk all round the edge without falling in. Well, what Kenny didn't realise was that the edge of the fountain was really slippery... As you can guess, Mrs Weaver wasn't too thrilled, and neither were the two gardeners, who came rushing to fish her out!

"Maybe that'll stop you from making bets now!" Frankie grinned as we all climbed back on to the minibus to go home.

Kenny ignored that. "I've just got to get that autograph!" she said gloomily. She was wearing Mrs Weaver's jumper because her sweatshirt had got soaked. "And now we've only got one day left."

"Let's hope the film crew are at Disneyland tomorrow," I agreed. "Otherwise the M&Ms are going to get one over on us, big time!"

CHAPTER NINE

"This is it then!" Frankie said grimly as we sat down at the back of the minibus the following morning. Breakfast had been even worse than usual, with the M&Ms going on and on about winning the bet.

"Yeah, but let's not spoil our day at Disneyland by worrying about the stupid M&Ms!" Kenny said, trying to be cheerful.

"Here they come now!" Lyndz said in a low voice.

The M&Ms were getting onto the minibus, talking in loud voices. They were really winding us up by discussing all the horrible things they were going to do when Kenny handed over her Leicester City autographs.

"I think I'll tear them up really slowly bit by bit!" the Queen was saying with a big grin on her face.

"Or we could use them as loo paper!" the Goblin giggled.

We ignored them, although Kenny was looking a bit sick at the thought of her precious autographs being used as bog roll! If the M&Ms did win the bet, which looked pretty likely now, we'd have to get used to them going on about it for the next ten years!

Almost everyone was on the coach, when to our surprise, Pascal climbed on.

"Hey, Pascal!" called Ryan Scott, who was sitting a few seats in front of us. "Come and sit with us, mate!"

Pascal made his way down the coach, grinning at Ryan and Danny. "My mother says I can come with you to Disneyland! No school for me today!"

"Nice one!" said Danny.

Pascal dumped his bag next to Ryan and Danny, but he didn't sit down. Instead he came down the coach towards us.

"I have some good news for you!" he whispered, looking sideways at the M&Ms to make sure they weren't listening.

"What?" Kenny asked. "Did Chantal smile today or something?"

"No, better than that!" Pascal winked at us. "My older brother works at Disneyland. He told me last night that an English film crew are going to shoot some scenes for a soap opera there today!"

"*What!*" we all screeched, hardly daring to believe our ears.

"Really cross-your-heart truly?" Fliss asked breathlessly.

"You're not playing another joke on us, are you?" Frankie asked.

Pascal shook his head. "No, they will be there. All you have to do is find them!"

"Oh, we will!" Kenny told him. "And when we do, I'm going to enjoy seeing the look on the M&Ms' faces!"

Pascal grinned, and went off to sit with Ryan and Danny. Well, that bit of news had *really* cheered us up! We all started bouncing up and down in our seats, talking at the tops of our voices and discussing what we were going to make the Queen and the Goblin do when we won the bet and they had to become our slaves!

"I'm going to make Emma Hughes carry all my luggage all the way home!" Frankie said with a grin.

"They can do all our packing as well as carry our bags!" Lyndz chimed in.

"And they can buy loads of chocolate for us!" Fliss added.

The Queen and the Goblin heard what we were saying. They turned round in their seats and stared haughtily at us. "No chance!" Emma Hughes said snootily. "Just get those Leicester City autographs ready for me as soon as we get home, Kenny!"

"That's what *you* think!" Kenny winked at us, and we all grinned. The Queen and the Goblin were in for the biggest shock of their lives!

But it was the Sleepover Club who were in for the shock...

"This is it!" Fliss announced as suddenly we all caught sight of a huge white building with a red roof. "This is Disneyland Paris!"

We all started cheering and whooping and giving each other high fives as Mr Tate drove into the car park. Then, before we could get off the minibus, Mrs Weaver did her usual lecture thing about behaving ourselves and not getting into trouble, but we weren't listening, of course! The only time we pricked up our ears was when she said we wouldn't be allowed to go round Disneyland on our own. We were all annoyed, but Mrs Weaver explained that kids weren't allowed on some of the rides without an adult. So we were all divided into three groups of five, and got one of the teachers to look after us. We got Mr Tate.

"Nice one!" Kenny said gleefully, giving the rest of us a thumbs-up. Mr Tate was OK, and much easier to fool than Mrs Weaver!

Then Mrs Weaver gave each of us a map, showing the five different 'Lands' inside the park. It was then that we started to get a bit worried.

"Hey, this place is enormous!" Frankie whispered.

"I didn't realise it was so big!" Kenny groaned, scanning the map anxiously. The five Lands were Frontierland, Adventureland, Fantasyland, Discoveryland and Main Street USA. The place was absolutely huge. How on earth were we going to know where the film crew were?

"Why didn't you say it was so big, Fliss?" I groaned.

"I didn't think." Fliss was looking as dismayed as the rest of us.

"Oh, well, we'll just have to do our best," Lyndz said hopefully. We all nodded. But we were feeling a bit depressed as we trailed off the minibus.

That didn't last long though! I mean, we were at *Disneyland*!

The big white building was the entrance,

and Fliss said it was a hotel where she and her family had stayed last time they visited. In front of the entrance were some pretty gardens, and there was a big Mickey Mouse face made out of flowers! We all cheered up when we saw that. We could hardly wait to get inside!

"Wow!" Frankie gasped as we walked into Main Street USA. "This is awesome!"

We were standing on a big white street, lined with big buildings. It looked like a scene from an old American film. Horse-drawn carts were taking people up and down the street, there were restaurants and shops, and Minnie Mouse and Donald Duck were walking around, shaking hands with people! Right at the end of the street was a huge fairytale castle with lots of turrets.

"That's Sleeping Beauty's Castle," Fliss said as we all looked at our maps to try and work out what it was. "It's the entrance to Fantasyland. Shall we go there first?"

"No, Adventureland first!" Kenny begged.

"No, Discoveryland!" said Frankie.

"Make your minds up!" said Mr Tate with a smile. So we decided on Fantasyland first.

We were all so excited, we forgot about the film crew for a while. We went into Fantasyland, and saw the dragon in his lair underneath Sleeping Beauty's Castle. We went on Captain Hook's pirate ship and flew to Never-Never Land. We went on a canal boat cruise through Storybook Land. We even had a ride on Dumbo! We didn't see the film crew, but we had a fab time.

"Right, Adventureland next!" Kenny said as we studied our maps to see which way we had to go.

"Just a minute!" Lyndz whispered suddenly. "I thought I just saw Danni Hart!"

"Where?" we all yelled.

"There!" Lyndz said, pointing. So we all rushed off in that direction.

"Hey! Adventureland is the other way!" Mr Tate shouted, running after us and waving his map in the air, but we ignored him!

So we ended up in Discoveryland. Of course, we just had to go on Space Mountain, even though we had to queue for ages. Space Mountain was brilliant! You sit strapped in on a rocket train, and then you go shooting up and down through space, and you see all kinds of things like asteroids and meteorite showers. It was awesome! Although Mr Tate looked a bit wobbly when we got off!

After that we went to Honey, I Shrunk The Audience. We had to queue up for ages for that as well, but it was worth it. It was brilliant, because we (the audience) were supposed to have shrunk and everything else was really big. My favourite bit was when this gi-normous dog stuck his head out into the audience!

"Right, it's time to meet the others for lunch," said Mr Tate, glancing at his watch. "Come on, we've got to go back to Main Street USA."

"And keep your eyes open for that film crew!" Frankie told us.

It took us a while to get back to Main Street because there was so much to look at, and Kenny insisted on having her photo taken with Baloo the Bear! When we finally made it, the others were waiting for us. The first thing we noticed was that the Queen and the Goblin were grinning fit to bust.

"What's up with them?" Frankie muttered. We soon found out.

"Oh no!" Fliss groaned. "*Look!*"

We looked down Main Street. There were the film crew. There was Danni Hart and the other actors – and they were just leaving!

"Oh no!" Kenny gasped. "We've missed them!"

"Yeah, you sure have!" Emily Berryman said between uproarious giggles, and she and the Queen laughed so much they could hardly stand. We all looked at each other in complete dismay.

"So much for winning that bet!" Kenny muttered gloomily. "I'm done for – and so are my autographs!"

"Hey, girls!" Pascal was standing with Ryan Scott and Danny McCloud, but when he spotted us, he came over. "I have something for you!"

He dived into his bag, and pulled out a piece of paper. Guess what it was!

CHAPTER TEN

"*It's Danni Hart's autograph!*" I yelled excitedly. Not only that – it was written on a colour publicity photo of Danni dressed up as her soap character Billie Johnson! 'Danni Hart as Billie Johnson' was written across the top, and it also had the *Westwood Street* logo printed on it. Danni had scrawled her signature at the bottom of the picture.

"Where did you get it, Pascal?" Frankie gabbled.

"*How* did you get it?" Fliss asked, her eyes wide.

"You're wicked, Pascal!" Lyndz exclaimed.

For once, Kenny was speechless. She just held out her hand and took the photo, staring at it as if she couldn't believe her eyes.

"I asked my brother to get it if he have a chance," Pascal grinned. "And he did!"

The M&Ms were looking over at us uncertainly, knowing something was going on, but not quite sure what!

"I don't believe it!" Kenny was looking completely dazed. "I just don't believe it!"

"Maybe we'd better let the M&Ms know right away!" Frankie nudged Kenny and winked.

Immediately Kenny went over to the Queen and the Goblin, keeping the photo out of sight behind her back, and we all followed, including Pascal. We weren't going to miss a minute of this!

"Er – Emma, can I talk to you for a minute?" Kenny said in a gloomy voice.

"What about?" the Queen asked, raising her eyebrows.

"Look, Emma, let's forget all about that

stupid bet, shall we?" Kenny said pleadingly, pretending to look all depressed. "It was daft. I shouldn't have done it."

"Forget about it? No way José!" Emma screeched. "We've won that bet fair and square, and I want those football autographs *and* your shirt when we get home!"

"You sure about that?" Kenny asked while the rest of us tried not to laugh.

"Positive!" Emma replied snootily.

"Well, that's a shame," Kenny said coolly. "Because I win!"

And she produced the photo from behind her back like a magician pulling a rabbit from a hat.

The Queen and the Goblin stared at it as if they were hypnotised.

"It – it can't be!" Emily spluttered.

"It's – it's a fake!" Emma roared. "It must be!"

"Oh, get real!" Frankie put in as Kenny shoved the photo right under Emma's nose. "The autograph's on an official *Westwood Street* publicity handout!"

We all looked smugly at the Queen and the Goblin, waiting for them to give in.

"How did you get it?" Emma demanded weakly.

"Doesn't matter," Kenny retorted. "The point is, we've got it, and that means…"

"You LOSE!" we all chorused, and then burst out laughing.

Purple in the face, the Queen and the Goblin turned away, but Kenny wasn't finished with them yet.

"Hold on, slaves!" she called. "We want a drink. Go and get us some Coke, will you? And hurry up about it!"

I've never seen two people look more like they were about to explode with fury! As the Queen and the Goblin stomped off, yelling at each other, we all cheered and slapped Pascal on the back.

"Thanks, mate!" Kenny said. "We couldn't have done it without you. I could kiss you – if I didn't hate boys!"

We all laughed, but Fliss looked quite keen!

"Right, now we've sorted out the M&Ms,

let's enjoy the rest of the day at Disneyland!"
I said firmly.

"Yeah, and we'll have a massive sleepover
tonight too!" Lyndz put in. And we all cheered
again!

"My favourite was Indiana Jones and the
Temple of Peril," Kenny said as she munched
a piece of cheese.

"Mine was Phantom Manor," said Lyndz.

Fliss shuddered. "Ooh, I didn't like that.
Mine was Honey, I Shrunk The Audience."

"I liked the Peter Pan thing best," I said,
grabbing the last doughnut.

"My favourite was Space Mountain."
Frankie leapt on me, trying to get the last bit
of doughnut, and I had to fight her off!

We'd got back from Disneyland, tired but
happy. We decided we'd buy Pascal a present
to say thanks, so we'd bought him the biggest
bar of chocolate we could find in the whole of
Disneyland. We were going to give it to him
the next day before we went home. Mrs
Weaver had told us to pack our bags after

dinner, so we'd got the Queen and the Goblin to help. They weren't very pleased! But they were our slaves until tomorrow, so it served them right.

Although we were all so tired, we'd managed to have a brilliant sleepover. We'd had a midnight feast and talked about Disneyland. Then we'd written all about Disneyland in our diaries. And after that, Kenny'd had the brilliant idea of acting out scenes from some of the Disney movies we'd seen. Now we were all yawning, although we didn't really want to go to bed just yet.

"This has been an *excellent* holiday," Kenny said through an enormous yawn. "What shall we do now?"

"Wake Fliss up – she's snoring!" Frankie said, and she poked Fliss in the back. "Hey! This sleepover isn't over yet!"

"I wasn't asleep!" Fliss sniffed, rubbing her eyes.

"It was really great of Pascal to get that autograph for us, wasn't it?" Lyndz remarked sleepily.

"Yes, maybe we should have invited him to the sleepover to say thank you," Fliss suggested.

We all began shouting at once!

"Boys at our sleepover! No way!" Kenny yelled.

"I'm not having a sleepover with boys!" Frankie exclaimed.

"Pascal's nice but he's not that nice!" I added.

"I think I've got hiccups!" Lyndz wailed. "Hic!"

We were just about to try out one of our fail-safe cures for Lyndz's hiccups, when we heard footsteps coming up the stairs.

"Quick, into bed!" Kenny whispered urgently, rushing to turn off the light.

We all dived under the duvets and pretended to be asleep in silence. Even Lyndz's hiccups had stopped – it must have been the shock! A few minutes later the door opened and we heard Mrs Weaver's voice say, "Is everything all right, girls?" When nobody answered, she went out and closed the door quietly.

We all lay there for about five minutes to give her a chance to go back downstairs, and then I sat up.

"Shall we sing our sleepover song now?" I asked. *"Down by the river there's a hanky-panky..."*

But no-one else joined in. All I could hear was the sound of deep breathing and Fliss snoring. They'd all gone to sleep! So I lay down and went to sleep myself.

We were so tired after the sleepover and all the excitement with the M&Ms that we could hardly get up the following morning. We were having breakfast early too because we were going home, so Mrs Weaver came banging on our door at seven o'clock. We managed to drag ourselves out of bed and downstairs, but we nearly fell asleep over our croissants!

"I hope we see Pascal before we leave," Lyndz said anxiously, as we stood outside the hotel while the teachers loaded up the minibus with our luggage.

"Hey, Emma!" Kenny called. "Put our bags on the coach, will you? And hurry up about it!"

The Queen and the Goblin stomped over and picked up our bags, their faces like thunder. We all started laughing.

"Ah, I am just in time to say goodbye!" Pascal came running down the stairs, pulling his jumper over his head.

"Thanks again, you were great!" Kenny beamed at him.

"And this is for you!" I said, handing him the big bar of chocolate.

Pascal looked pleased. "*Merci*. Thank you." Then he lowered his voice. "But I have a little secret to tell you…"

We all gathered round him curiously.

"That autograph," Pascal began. "It is not Danni Hart's!"

We were all so shocked we couldn't say anything at first.

"But – but you've got the official publicity photo!" Frankie stammered.

Pascal nodded. "My brother got that from the film crew. He asked Danni Hart for her signature, but she was in a bad mood and she didn't do it!"

"So whose signature is it?" Kenny whipped out the photo and studied it carefully.

"I asked my brother to sign it 'Danni Hart'!" Pascal whispered.

We all glanced at the minibus. The Queen and the Goblin were staggering on to it, carrying our luggage and arguing bitterly. We all howled with laughter.

"That makes it even better!" Kenny said triumphantly. "Thanks, Pascal!"

Pascal winked at us. "I will not say goodbye, I will say '*Au revoir*'. That means we will meet again sometime!"

So that was the story of our holiday in Paris – and how we discovered that some boys aren't all that bad! The M&Ms still haven't forgiven us, so I bet they'll be out for revenge sometime soon... but we'll be ready for them!

See ya! I mean, *au revoir*!

28

Sleepover Club Eggstravaganza

Yum! It's Easter, and time for an All Chocolate Sleepover! Not to mention Frankie's little sister Izzy's naming party. For a laugh, Frankie takes some of her old baby pics into school to show the Sleepover Club, but disaster strikes when the M&Ms get hold of them... and a messy revenge means serious trouble for the gang. Easter bunnies? Easter funnies, more like!

Stock up on chocs
for an egg-cellent time!

Emergency Sleepover

High drama! Rosie has an accident, and is whisked away to Queen Mary's Hospital in an ambulance. Is it all Kenny's fault? Fliss seems to think so... But Rosie recovers, and the girls plan some fund-raising for the children's ward. Chaos comes to Cuddington with a scavenger hunt, a mufti day at school – and Kenny in a very large bath of baked beans...

Rattle those tins and collect some cash!

Order Form

To order direct from the publishers, just make a list of the titles you want and fill in the form below:

Name ....

Address ....

....

....

Send to: Dept 6, HarperCollins Publishers Ltd, Westerhill Road, Bishopbriggs, Glasgow G64 2QT.

Please enclose a cheque or postal order to the value of the cover price, plus:

UK & BFPO: Add £1.00 for the first book, and 25p per copy for each additional book ordered.

Overseas and Eire: Add £2.95 service charge. Books will be sent by surface mail but quotes for airmail despatch will be given on request.

A 24-hour telephone ordering service is available to holders of Visa, MasterCard, Amex or Switch cards on 0141- 772 2281.

Collins
An *Imprint* of HarperCollins*Publishers*